Introducing Miss Witchy Effie Leffy

by Vennard Wright

In Enchantwood Jungle, where dreams intertwine,
Lived Witchy Effie Leffy, who always seemed fine.
Her hair shone bright, like midnight curls, glistening and black in endless twirls.

1

Miss Witchy's best friend was named Mrs. Mungle. Her laughter and spells helped rule the jungle. With talking critters, and trees in bright dress,
In daylit sparkles, their paths effervesce.

2

Every day, with the dawn's first light,
They'd set off on adventures always in sight.
Spreading kindness, far and wide,
To strangers and beasts, side by side.

3

Miss Witchy Effie Leffy lived in tree cottage, next to Mrs. Mungle with colors high wattage.

Over time they worked very hard,
to adorn their houses with
crystals and shards.

Inside their homes, the shelves were full of books, with lots of cabinets and small, secret nooks.

6

The two friends spent their days casting spells, spreading much joy and painting snail shells.

One sunny morning they went to
find corn and found a family of
squirrels who lost their acorns.

With a sprinkle of kindness and a dash of their magic, they found the acorns in a nearby house attic.

The grateful squirrels all chattered with joy, and thanked the two friends with a shiny new toy.

As the days passed, way deep in the woods, word spread of the friends who would always do good.

They helped the animals, and tended the trees, while filling their bellies with honey from bees.

12

Their laughter always echoed in spurts as mystical creatures appeared in silk skirts.

The two friends, were quite dear indeed, with magic to spare, for those in need.

Sometimes they would create a ridiculous rhyme where Miss Witchy turns young and Mrs. Mungle lost time.

15

In a realm so odd, where things
play and nod,
Lived Miss Witchy Effie Leffy,
her spirit seemed awed.
Her comrade, Mrs. Mungle, in the
jungle's embrace,
Where creatures would juggle,
and tadpoles find space.

16

One day Miss Witchy, feeling whimsy so twitchy,
Spoke to Mrs. Mungle, "Let's make life more pitchy!
Forget the stern rules in our magical schools,
Dive into nonsense like whimsical fools."

Mrs. Mungle went to the jungle
to buy a jar of tar,
She spied a stump, tried to
jump, but fell in a trolley car.
It twirled and it spun, a ride
under the sun,
Through the jungle it danced,
the laughter had begun.

The trolley was jolly, with a bell
that went dolly,
Mrs. Mungle laughed, her spirits
so volley.
No worries, no cares, just
laughter in pairs,
Zipping through the jungle,
escaping all snares.

19

Back in their town, with smiles,
no frowns to be found,
Miss Witchy, Mrs. Mungle,
whimsical gowns they'd don.
They taught the young to laugh
without end,
Embrace the absurd, cherish each
friend.

20

In this strange land, whimsy
grand,
Miss Witchy Effie Leffy and
Mrs. Mungle took a stand.
In nonsense and fun, a lesson
spun,
Joy and laughter should always
be won.

In this realm of delight, where
dreams take flight,
Children learn without fear, in a
world shining bright.
No shadows of worry, no rush, no
hurry,
In schools of laughter, innocence
won't bury.

22

No echoes of shots, just giggles in lots,
Painting dreams on creative thought spots.
A whimsical place, kindness takes space,
Aimed only at smiles on each face.

23

So, let's weave a spell, where all children dwell,
In a haven of learning, where joy and love swell.
No need for alarms, just warmth and charms,
In a future where no firearm harms.

24

So declares Miss Witchy Effie
Leffy, with whimsical charms...

The End!

25

Made in the USA
Middletown, DE
15 January 2024

47910245R00015